HEDGEHOG'S TALKING TREE

BY LUCY KINCAID

ILLUSTRATED BY PAMELA STOREY

BRIMAX BOOKS · NEWMARKET · ENGLAND

Bob Hedgehog likes to talk. He has a lot to say. He talks about the flowers. He talks about the trees. He talks about the sky. He talks about things he has done. He is always talking. He goes on and on talking.

Bob Hedgehog finds a stone. It has a hole in it. He wants to talk about the stone. He sees Little Hamster.

Little Hamster is digging. "I want to tell you about my stone," says Bob Hedgehog.

Little Hamster is busy. He does not want to stop. "Tell me later," says Little Hamster.

Bob Hedgehog sees Polly Pig.
Polly Pig is washing.
"I want to tell you about my stone," says Bob Hedgehog.
Polly Pig is busy. She does not want to stop.
"Tell me later," says Polly Pig.

Bob Hedgehog sees
Cheepy Chick.
Cheepy Chick is dusting.
"I want to tell you about
my stone," says Bob
Hedgehog.
Cheepy Chick is busy. She
does not want to stop.
"Tell me later," says
Cheepy Chick.

No one will listen. They are all too busy.

Bob Hedgehog sees a tree. "I want to tell you about my stone," says Bob Hedgehog.

The tree is not busy. The tree does not say, "Tell me later."

So, Bob Hedgehog tells the tree about his stone.

"I will tell all the trees,"
says Bob Hedgehog.
His friends see him talking
to the trees.
"Shall we play a trick?"
says Little Hamster.
"Yes," says Polly Pig.

Little Hamster hides behind a tree. Bob Hedgehog talks to the tree.

"I want to tell you about my stone," says Bob Hedgehog.

"What do you want to tell me?" says Little Hamster. Bob Hedgehog thinks the tree is talking.

Bob Hedgehog looks around. He must tell someone about the talking tree. There is no one to tell. He tells the next tree. "That tree can talk," he says.

Polly Pig is hiding behind the tree. "So can I," says Polly Pig.

Bob Hedgehog thinks that the tree is talking.

"I must tell someone,"
says Bob Hedgehog.
He sees Cheepy Chick.
He runs to her.
"Come with me," he says.
Cheepy Chick is busy. She
is sweeping. She does not
want to stop.
"Come with me," says Bob
Hedgehog. Cheepy Chick
has to go.

"That tree can talk," says Bob Hedgehog.
"Trees cannot talk," says Cheepy Chick.
"Say something, tree," says Bob Hedgehog.
The tree says nothing.
"I am going home," says Cheepy Chick.
"Wait," says Bob Hedgehog.

Bob Hedgehog takes Cheepy Chick to the next tree.

"That tree can talk," he says. "Say something, tree."

The tree says nothing.

"Are you playing a trick on me?" asks Cheepy Chick.

"No," says Bob Hedgehog. He shakes his head. "It must have been a dream," he says.

Little Hamster is hiding behind the tree.
"It was not a dream," says Little Hamster.
Bob Hedgehog thinks it is the tree talking.
"I told you trees can talk," says Bob Hedgehog.
Cheepy Chick knows trees cannot talk. She goes behind the tree. She sees Little Hamster.

"It was Little Hamster talking," says Cheepy Chick.
"I was playing a trick on you," says Little Hamster.
Polly Pig comes out. "So was I," she says.
Bob Hedgehog says nothing.
He just does not know what to say.

Say these words again

things	listen
talking	always
dream	does
stone	nothing
busy	thinks
trick	shakes
behind	know